COSMO'S MOON

Written by Devin Scillian and Illustrated by Mark Braught

Sleeping Bear Press

Cosmo
loved
the moon.

He had moon pajamas

and a moon night-light and stars

and moons all over his bedroom.

Every night, Cosmo's mother and father

gave him a hug and a kiss

and tucked him into his bed.

But just as soon

as they closed his bedroom door,

he threw aside the covers,

ran to the open window,

and watched as the golden moon

came into the night sky

just above the sycamore tree.

And as a gentle night breeze

blew across the curtains,

Cosmo would talk and the moon would listen.

Some nights,

Cosmo would tell the moon

the funniest stories and his happiest dreams.

Some nights,

Cosmo would tell the moon about sad things.

And like best friends always do,

the moon listened to those, too.

Some nights before going to bed,
Cosmo would take a walk in the moonlight.
And no matter where he walked,
it looked to Cosmo as if the moon
were following him.

"I think the moon is following me,"

he said one evening.

"I know," said his mother.

"It fools us that way.

It's because the moon is so very big."

"Not exactly," said his father.

"It's because the moon is so very far away."

"Actually, it's both," said his grandfather,

holding a large coin in front of Cosmo's nose.

"It's because the moon is so very big

and yet so very far away."

But Cosmo wasn't so sure.

Lately the moon seemed

to be just behind him all the time.

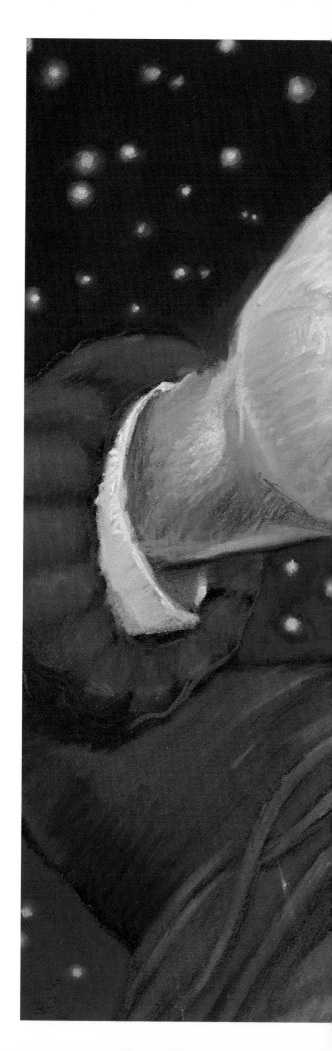

When he was eating breakfast.

While he was at recess.

While he was on his way home from school.

And at his Little League baseball games.

For Cosmo, it was always nighttime.

And the day his family sat down for a picnic lunch

under the glow of the giant moon,

barely able to see the piece of cheese in his hand,

his father finally asked,

"Where in the world is the sun?

The moon seems to be out

at the oddest times lately."

"I told you, Father," said Cosmo.

"I think the moon is following me."

His family stared at him.

But, yes, the more they thought about it,

the more they realized that

Cosmo never seemed to be without his moon.

"How strange," said his father.

"How odd," said his mother.

"How wonderful," said his grandfather,

and he gave Cosmo a hug

and told him he must be a special boy.

Sometimes it was difficult to know

just when to go to bed.

And it was almost impossible to wake up on time.

But slowly the family got used to the constant glow

of Cosmo's moon.

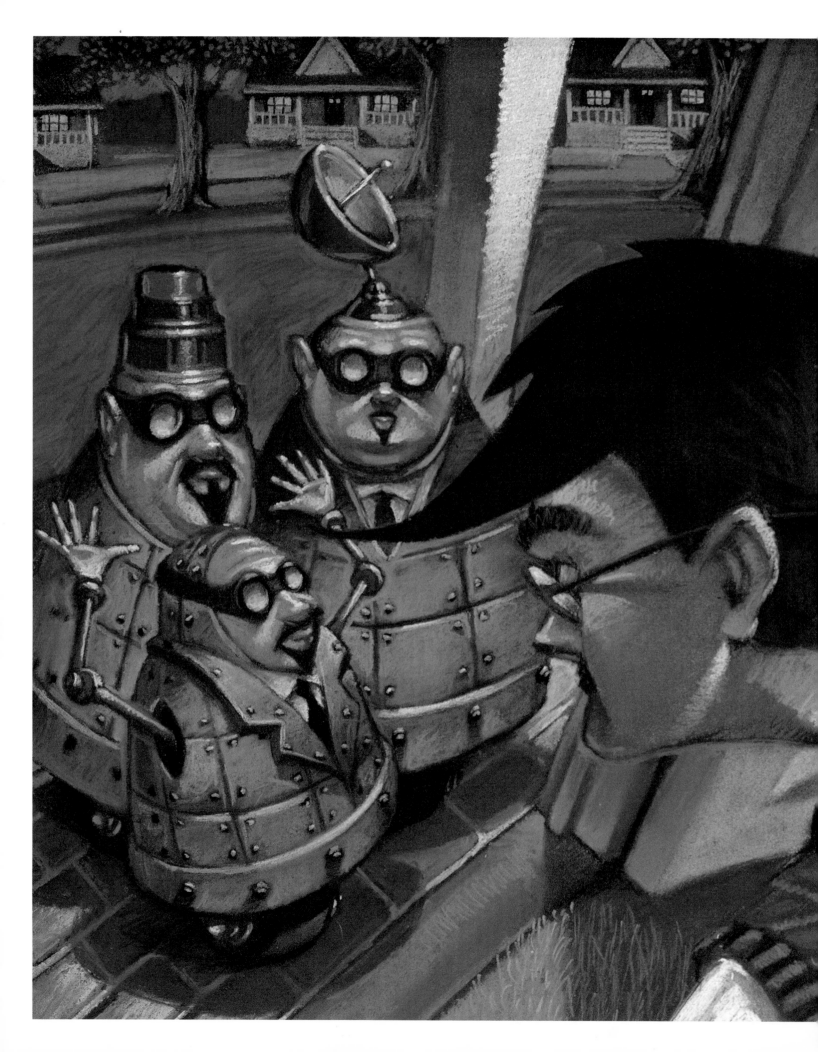

Until one night

there was a knock at the door.

It was a group of astronomers

who wanted to know why

after millions of years

the moon had changed its ways.

They had spent days and days

peering into their telescopes

and believed the boy

who lived at 29 Luna Lane

had something to do

with the moon's behavior.

"It's confusing the oceans," said one.

"The tides can't come in without the moon."

"It's confusing the flowers," said the second.

"The morning glories never get any sun, so they never bloom."

"And it's confusing the dogs," said the third.

"Listen to that racket."

Indeed,

dogs were howling all over town,

howling at the moon that never left the sky.

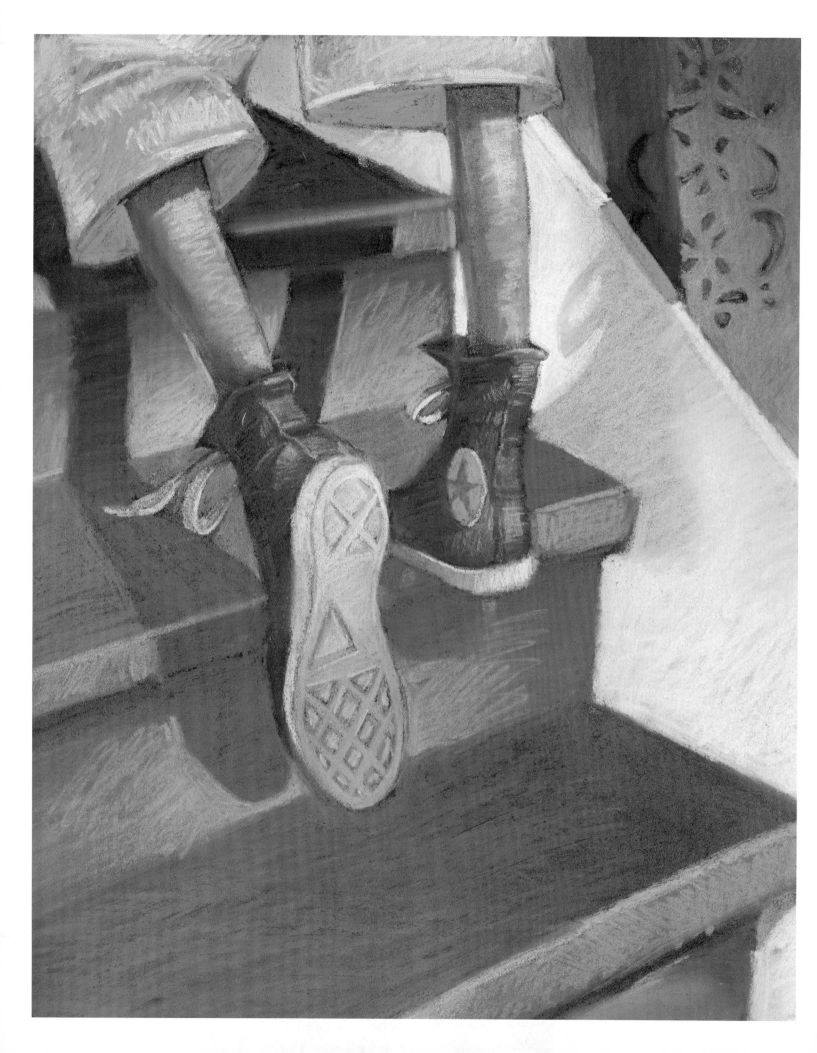

"Surely you're not suggesting

Cosmo has anything to do with it," said Cosmo's father.

"That's exactly what we're suggesting," said one.

"Perhaps a giant ray gun on the roof."

"Or an ultramagnetic stealth beam from a radio!"

"How diabolical!" said another.

"That's absurd!" said Cosmo's father.

"The question is," said the first, glaring at Cosmo,

"why is the moon following you?"

"I'm not sure," said Cosmo. "I'll ask him."

"Ask him?" laughed the astronomers.

"You're going to ask the moon?"

They thought it was terribly funny.

But Cosmo climbed the stairs to his room

and leaned out his bedroom window.

"You've been following me," said Cosmo.

And the moon seemed to blush.

"Yes," said the moon. "I have."

"But why?" asked Cosmo.

The moon beamed.

"Because you're good and kind.

You talk to me," said the moon.

"And I know I make you happy.

So I wanted you to be happy all the time,

not just during the evenings."

"Gosh, that's nice," said Cosmo.

And for a moment

they just sat, enjoying each other's company.

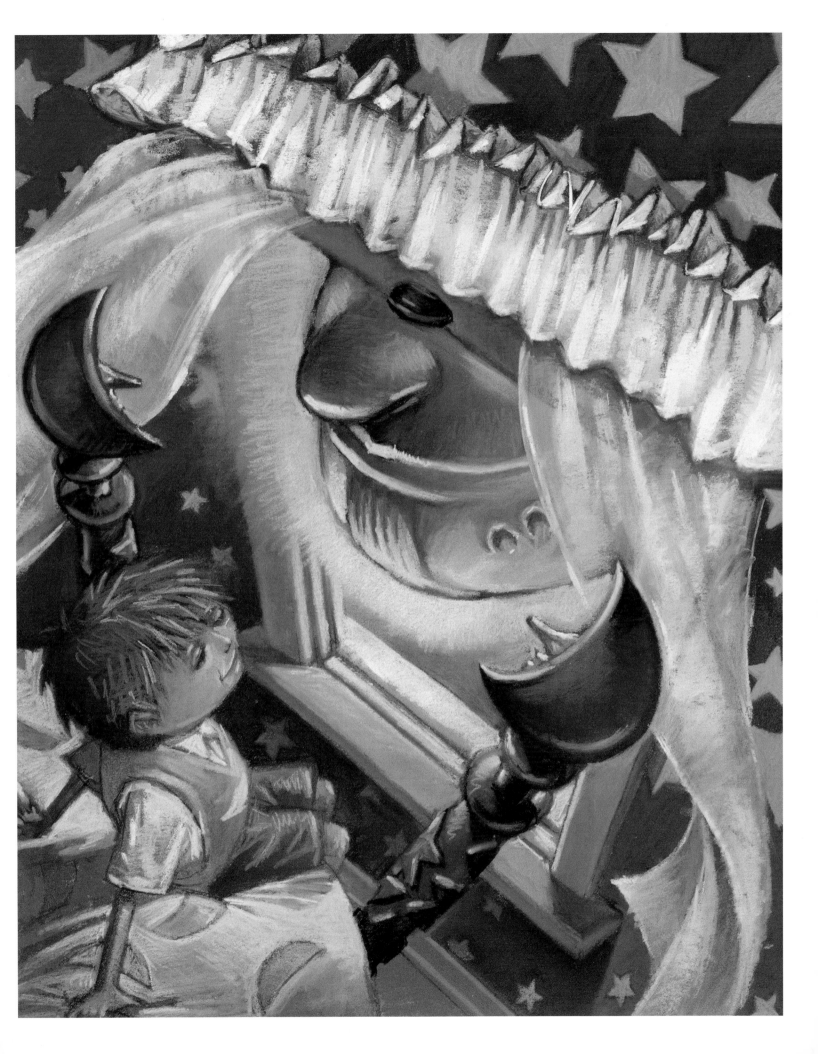

Finally, Cosmo said,

"It's wonderful, really.

But the ocean tides are lost without you."

"I didn't realize," said the moon.

"And the morning glories never bloom."

"I hadn't thought of that, either," the moon answered.

"And the dogs are making an awful racket."

"I do know that," said the moon.

And they listened to the howls from up and down the street.

"But don't you want me with you?"

asked the moon.

"Of course," said Cosmo.

"But you know what the best part is?

It's watching you come up each night,

the way you appear at the end of the day.

But now you're always there.

I guess I miss that part."

"That's a lovely thing to say," said the moon.

And they both stared into the branches of the sycamore.

"I guess never saying goodbye
means you never get to say hello,"

said the moon,

and he looked to the faraway oceans

and smiled at the morning glories patiently waiting to bloom.

"You'll still be here? And you'll talk to me?" he asked.

"Every night," said Cosmo.

"I'll be waiting right here."

The astronomers were still laughing
when Cosmo came down the stairs.
And when he told them that the moon
had agreed to return to its orbit,
they laughed even louder,
until a gentle beam of sunlight
broke on the horizon
and shined through the doorway.
And so the tides returned
to their to-and-fro against the sand.
The morning glories again bloomed
in the morning sun.
And the dogs returned their attention
to burying bones
and chasing the neighborhood cats.

But every once in a while,

you'll see the moon quietly sneak into the daytime sky.

Those are the days when the moon

wants to spend just a little extra time with Cosmo,

the little boy who loved him most of all.

For Doc and Joenne, who gave me the greatest gift of all...their daughter.

—DEVIN SCILLIAN

For Hannah, Ben, Melle, Jack, & Grant

—MARK BRAUGHT

Text copyright © 2003 Devin Scillian
Illustration copyright © 2003 Mark Braught

Sleeping Bear Press
310 North Main Street
Chelsea, MI 48118
www.sleepingbearpress.com

Sleeping Bear Press is an imprint of The Gale Group, Inc.,
a division of Thomson Learning, Inc.

Printed and bound in Canada.

10 9 8 7 6 5 4 3 2 1

Library of Congress Cataloging-in-Publication Data
Scillian, Devin.
Cosmo's moon / written by Devin Scillian ; illustrated by Mark Braught.
p. cm.
Summary: After Cosmo's affection for the Moon causes it to leave its orbit and begin to follow him around,
he must reassure the Moon that saying goodbye makes the hello even sweeter.
ISBN 1-58536-123-2
[1. Moon—Fiction. 2. Night—Fiction. 3. Bedtime—Fiction.]
I. Braught, Mark, ill. II. Title.
PZ7.S41269 Co 2003
[E]--dc21
2003002195